No Peeking at Presents

No Peeking at Presents

by
Alastair Heim

Illustrated by
Sara Not

Clarion Books • *An Imprint of* HarperCollins*Publishers*

There.
Everything looks perfectly merry.
But now it is time for bed.
And you both know
the **number one rule**
on Christmas Eve . . .

There is **no peeking at presents** before Mommy and Daddy wake up.

Now then . . . good night.

3:00 a.m.

SQUEAK

What are you
two doing???

Maybe it was just your imagination.

Do you know what I think?
I think that maybe, just **MAYBE,**
you both forgot tonight's **number one rule.**

There is **no peeking** at presents.

Now. To make sure you don't try to peek **AGAIN**, I will sleep downstairs until Mommy and Daddy wake up. Good night.

But we really **DID** hear a—

I said, **GOOD NIGHT.**

Two Hours Later . . .
5:00 a.m.

you're doing?

Maybe it was
a **MOUSE**.

But I'm scared of mice!

Then you'd better get
back to bed.

Who do they think they're fooling?

There is **no peeking at presents.**

One Hour and Seventeen Minutes Later . . .
6:17 a.m.

at Presents!

Three minutes later . . .
6:20 a.m.

There **IS** no peeking
at presents . . .

. . . unless the present peeks
at **YOU** first!

SQUEAK!

WOOF!

WOOF!

WOOF!

For Mike, Sheila, Lyndsey, and Ellie...a true gift to our family
—A.H.

To sweet little Sunny, whose big ears and
champagne-colored fur make us smile every day
—S.N.

Clarion Books is an imprint of HarperCollins Publishers.

No Peeking at Presents
Text copyright © 2022 by Alastair Heim
Illustrations copyright © 2022 by Sara Not

ISBN 978-1-32-880959-9

The artist used pen, ink, and Photoshop to create the illustrations for this book.
Typography by Bones Leopard
22 23 24 25 26 RTLO 10 9 8 7 6 5 4 3 2 1

First Edition